Sports Illustrated KID$

STARS OF SPORTS

MOOKIE BETTS

BASEBALL CHAMPION

by Matt Chandler

CAPSTONE PRESS

a capstone imprint

Published by Capstone Press, an imprint of Capstone
1710 Roe Crest Drive, North Mankato, Minnesota 56003
capstonepub.com

Library of Congress Cataloging-in-Publication Data is available on the Library of Congress website.
ISBN: 9781666347272 (hardcover)
ISBN: 9781666347289 (ebook PDF)

Summary: Mookie Betts started playing baseball as a child and has never looked back. Betts made his major-league baseball debut in 2014. In 2018, he won the American League MVP award and helped lead the Red Sox to a World Series win. In 2020, he helped lead the Dodgers to a World Series win. The top slugger and star fielder has also earned five Gold Glove Awards and four Silver Slugger Awards. Get the highlights of Betts's amazing career.

Editorial Credits
Editor: Carrie Sheely; Designer: Bobbie Nuytten; Media Researcher: Morgan Walters; Production Specialist: Polly Fisher

Image Credits
Associated Press: Kirby Lee, 27, Lynne Sladky, 19, Mike Janes, 11; Getty Images: Jim McIsaac, 14, 15, MediaNews Group/Boston Herald via Getty Images, 17, Meg Oliphant, 28, Norm Hall, 23, Portland Press Herald, 13, Robert Gauthier, 9, Ronald Martinez, 24, Sean M. Haffey, 5; Newscom: Jim Ruymen/UPI, Cover, 7; Shutterstock: Artbox, 8, David Lee, 1; Sports Illustrated: Erick W. Rasco, 20, 25, Robert Beck, 21

Source Notes
Pg. 6, "She would go . . . " "Betts Inherited Baseball Acumen from Dedicated Mom," MLB, May 8, 2015, https://www.mlb.com/news/red-sox-outfielder-mookie-betts-inherited-baseball-acumen-from-dedicated-mom/c-122752222, Accessed December 2021

Pg. 22, "I had initially . . . " "Dodgers' Mookie Betts: I Thought I Was Going to Be with Red Sox for Life," Bleacher Report, October 27, 2020, https://bleacherreport.com/articles/2915371-dodgers-mookie-betts-i-thought-i-was-going-to-be-with-red-sox-for-life, Accessed December 2021

All internet sites appearing in back matter were available and accurate when this book was sent to press.

TABLE OF CONTENTS

Words in **BOLD** are in the glossary.

WORLD SERIES WINNER

The Los Angeles Dodgers and the Tampa Bay Rays faced off in the 2020 World Series. Game 1 was a close battle with the Dodgers holding a 2–1 lead in the fifth inning. Dodgers' superstar Mookie Betts led off the inning with a walk. He easily stole second base. With slugger Justin Turner at the plate, Betts took off again. He dove headfirst into third base, beating the tag. The crowd at Dodger Stadium cheered wildly.

The next batter, Max Muncy, hit a **chopper** to first base. Betts raced toward home plate. He slid to the outside of the plate and swiped it with his hand. The umpire signaled safe! Betts's incredible speed brought in a run. Betts hit a home run later in the game. The Dodgers won the game 8–3. Strong hitting from Betts in later games helped the Dodgers go on to win the World Series.

>>> Betts slides into home plate during Game 1 of the 2020 World Series.

CHAPTER 1

EARLY SUCCESS

Markus Lynn "Mookie" Betts was born on October 7, 1992, in Tennessee. Today, Betts is known as one of the fastest players in baseball. His parents, Willie and Diana, say their son has been fast since he was a little boy.

Betts credits his mom with his early success on the baseball diamond. "She would go out and throw," Betts said in an interview. "Whatever sport it was, she would go out and play with me and I remember sometimes we used to race almost every day."

Diana became Betts's first coach when he was just 5 years old. She took him to sign up for Little League, and she was told he was too small to play. Instead of giving up, Diana formed her own team by inviting all the players other teams didn't want.

>>> Betts hugs his mother, Diana, before the start of a 2021 game while his father, Willie, stands next to them.

FACT

Betts's parents dreamed their son would someday play major-league baseball. They even chose his name, Markus Lynn Betts, to form the initials MLB. His nickname Mookie came from his parents' love of watching professional basketball player Mookie Blaylock.

HIGH SCHOOL ATHLETE

When Betts reached John Overton High School in Nashville, he was a three-sport athlete. He was a baseball infielder and outfielder. He was a starting point guard on his high school basketball team. Betts was also a member of his high school bowling team. In 2010, Betts was named the Boys Bowler of the Year in Tennessee.

But it was baseball that made Betts the superstar he is today. His baseball coaches at Overton remember him as the most talented player on the team. As a senior, Betts hit an incredible .509 at the plate. Though he was an infielder, Betts even pitched a little. His high school coach Robert Morrison said Betts's pitches could reach 96 miles per hour.

Pro Bowler

Betts's mom loved to bowl. She took her son bowling often as a child. Betts became a talented bowler. He won his first tournament when he was only 8 years old. He was an excellent bowler in high school as well. Betts went on to compete professionally. In 2017, he rolled a perfect game in the qualifying round of the World Series of Bowling.

>>> Betts's determination and willingness to work on his skills helped make him into the star player he is today.

CHAPTER 2
MINOR-LEAGUE STAR

During his senior year at Overton, Betts had a decision to make. He accepted a **scholarship** to play baseball for the University of Tennessee. But then, the Boston Red Sox selected him in the 2011 Major League Baseball (MLB) **Draft**. Betts had to choose between a college education or getting paid to play baseball. The Red Sox offered him $750,000 to sign with the organization. Betts decided to withdraw his acceptance letter to attend the University of Tennessee. Even though he was only 18 years old, Betts was going to become a professional baseball player!

〉〉〉 Betts trains with the
Red Sox in Florida in
October 2011.

Most baseball players don't join a major-league team right away. Every major-league baseball team has several minor-league teams. Players start in these teams to develop their skills. Most players in the minor leagues never make it to the major leagues.

Betts was different. Betts began his career playing for a Red Sox minor-league team in Florida. His talent helped him rise through the Red Sox system quickly. He played for seven minor-league teams in four seasons. Betts drove in more than 150 runs in the minors. He also showed off his speed, stealing 92 bases. Betts was named to the 2014 All-Star Futures Game. The Red Sox decided he was ready to play major-league baseball.

FACT

After two years in the minor leagues, Betts wanted to quit the game. He thought he wasn't good enough. But instead of quitting, he worked even harder.

〉〉〉 Betts throws to first base to get a double play while on the minor-league Portland Sea Dogs team in 2014.

ROOKIE SEASON

It was June 29, 2014. More than 48,000 fans packed Yankee Stadium. The New York Yankees were playing their **rivals**, the Boston Red Sox. Betts was making his major-league **debut.** Facing pitcher Chase Whitley in the fourth inning, Betts swung at a fastball and slapped a single to center field. He had his first big-league hit!

⟩⟩⟩ Betts at bat during his debut MLB game

Betts played in 52 games as a **rookie**. He delivered 55 hits. Betts hit five home runs and stole seven bases. He also played 14 games at second base.

The Red Sox soon switched Betts to the outfield. The team had an All-Star second baseman, Dustin Pedroia. Coaches also thought Betts's speed would make him a great center fielder.

〉〉〉 Betts slides and reaches for a base during his debut MLB game.

CHAPTER 3
BECOMING A SUPERSTAR

Betts began the 2015 season as the starting center fielder. In the first Red Sox home game, he had one of his biggest games of the season. In the first inning, Washington Nationals superstar Bryce Harper crushed a ball deep. Betts raced back. He leaped high and caught the ball over the wall. He robbed Harper of a two-run home run.

Betts came to bat in the bottom of the second inning with two runners on base. He swung hard at a fastball and crushed a three-run homer to left field. The Red Sox went on to win the game 9–4.

It was the start of a good season for Betts. He hit 18 home runs and drove in 77 runs in his first full season in the major leagues.

〉〉〉 Betts reaches over the wall to catch the ball that Bryce Harper hit on April 13, 2015.

In 2016, Betts did even better. He hit 31 home runs and drove in 113 runs. He stole 26 bases. In the field, he recorded 14 **outfield assists**, the third most in the American League. He won his first Gold Glove Award. The Gold Glove is given each season to the best defensive players at each position.

His improved play also led to the Red Sox making the **playoffs**. But once in the playoffs, Betts had only two hits. The Red Sox were swept three games to none against Cleveland.

Betts had another strong season for the Red Sox in 2017. He drove in more than 100 runs for the second year in a row. He was named to his second All-Star Game and won his second Gold Glove Award.

Betts greets his teammates at the All-Star Game in July 2017.

MVP SEASON

In 2018, Betts had an incredible year. His batting average of .346 was the best in the major leagues. He also led the major leagues in runs scored with 129. Betts stole 30 bases, the most in his major-league career. He was named to the All-Star Game and won another Gold Glove. The Red Sox advanced to the playoffs. Betts's playoff performance wasn't as good as it was in the regular season. But the Red Sox still made it to the World Series.

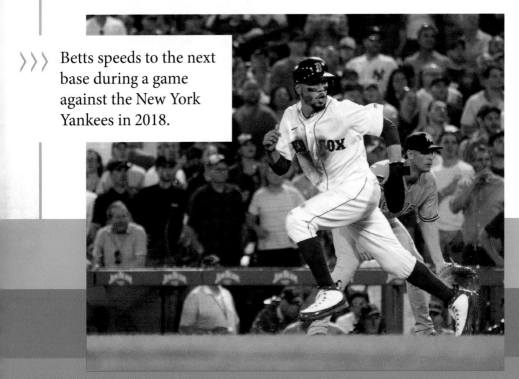

》》》 Betts speeds to the next base during a game against the New York Yankees in 2018.

The Red Sox faced the Los Angeles Dodgers in the World Series. In Game 5, Betts smashed a home run, crushing the Dodgers' hopes to make a comeback. The Red Sox defeated the Dodgers to win the 2018 World Series. Betts finished his season by winning the American League Most Valuable Player (MVP) Award.

〉〉〉 Betts at bat during Game 4 of the 2018 World Series

CHAPTER 4

WEST COAST TRADE

Betts had another strong season in 2019. He hit 29 home runs and led the team in stolen bases with 16. He also won another Gold Glove. After the season, Betts was set to become a **free agent**. The Red Sox knew Betts would want more than $300 million in a new contract. The team made the decision to trade Betts and get as many players as they could in return.

In February 2020, the team traded Betts to the Los Angeles Dodgers. "I had initially thought that I was going to be a Red Sox for life," Betts said in 2020. "But you know, God always has a plan for things."

>>> Betts attends spring training camp after being traded to the Dodgers in 2020.

SHORT-SEASON SUCCESS

Because of **COVID-19**, Major League Baseball shortened the 2020 season. Betts's batting average was .292 and he crushed 16 home runs in the short season. He also led the Dodgers to the best record in the major leagues.

Betts didn't stop there. In the first two rounds of the playoffs, Betts's batting average was .368. The Dodgers were soon on their way to the 2020 World Series.

〉〉〉 Betts reaches for a fly ball during Game 7 of the National League Championship Series in 2020.

>>> Betts slides into second base during Game 1 of the 2020 World Series.

The Dodgers faced the Tampa Bay Rays in the World Series. Once again, Betts showed why he is a former MVP. He delivered seven hits, including two home runs in the series. He also stole four bases and drove in three runs. The Dodgers topped the Rays four games to two, winning the World Series.

A Big Contract

In July 2020, the Dodgers signed Betts to a 12-year contract extension. The contract is worth $365 million. It will pay the superstar an average of $30.4 million per year. The deal is major-league baseball's second largest contract in total dollars.

CHAPTER 5

FUTURE IN LOS ANGELES

Baseball fans have debated whether the Dodgers made the right move to give Betts $365 million. Some think the team overpaid for a player that is hitting under .300 for his career. He has only driven in 100 runs twice in a season. Betts has only two 30-home-run seasons. But Betts is still a star player, and he is a fan favorite in Los Angeles. In 2021, his jersey was the highest selling of any player in baseball!

Betts has fallen in love with Los Angeles. He lives just outside of the city. He volunteers at many charity events in the community. He has also volunteered to help those in need during the COVID-19 pandemic.

FACT

Dodgers fans bought a billboard outside of Fenway Park in Boston to "thank" the Red Sox for trading Betts to Los Angeles.

>>> Betts helps hand out food to people in Los Angeles in November 2021.

WHAT DOES THE FUTURE HOLD?

Betts is one of the biggest superstars in the game. He has won two World Series rings. He is an All-Star and won the 2018 MVP Award. Although Betts is getting older, he has worked hard to stay in shape and play at the highest level. In 2021, he helped lead the Dodgers back to the National League Championship Series. Dodgers fans expect Betts will help bring even more championships to Los Angeles. If he keeps up his strong play, Betts may one day be elected to the Baseball Hall of Fame.

>>> Betts high-fives with kids after winning a game in 2021.

TIMELINE

1992 Markus Lynn "Mookie" Betts is born in Nashville, Tennessee, on October 7.

2011 The Boston Red Sox select Betts in the fifth round of the Major League Baseball Draft.

2014 Betts makes his major-league debut on June 29 against the New York Yankees.

2018 Betts wins his first World Series ring with the Boston Red Sox.

2018 Betts wins the American League Most Valuable Player Award.

2020 Betts wins his second World Series ring with the Los Angeles Dodgers.

2020 Betts wins his fifth Gold Glove in a row.

GLOSSARY

CHOPPER (CHOP-ur)—a high-bouncing batted baseball

COVID-19 (KO-vid nine-TEEN)—a mild to severe respiratory illness that is caused by a coronavirus

DEBUT (DAY-byoo)—a player's first game

DRAFT (DRAFT)—an event in which athletes are picked to join sports organizations or teams

FREE AGENT (FREE AY-juhnt)—a player who is free to sign with any team

OUTFIELD ASSIST (AUT-feeld uh-SIST)—when an outfielder throws the ball to the infield and an out occurs as a result

PLAYOFFS (PLAY-awfs)—a series of games played after the regular season to determine a champion

RIVAL (RYE-vuhl)—someone whom a person or team competes against

ROOKIE (RUK-ee)—a first-year player

SCHOLARSHIP (SKOL-ur-ship)—money given to a student to pay for school

READ MORE

Chandler, Matt. *Baseball's Greatest Walk-Offs and Other Crunch-Time Heroics*. North Mankato, MN: Capstone, 2021.

Fishman, Jon M. *Mookie Betts*. Minneapolis: Lerner Publications, 2020.

Flynn, Brendan. *Los Angeles Dodgers: All-Time Greats*. Mendota Heights, MN: North Star Editions, 2021.

INTERNET SITES

Baseball Reference: Mookie Betts
baseball-reference.com/players/b/bettsmo01.shtml

Kiddle: Mookie Betts Facts for Kids
kids.kiddle.co/Mookie_Betts

Major League Baseball: Mookie Betts #50
mlb.com/player/mookie-betts-605141

INDEX

AUTHOR BIO

Matt Chandler is the author of more than 60 books for children and thousands of articles published in newspapers and magazines. He writes mostly nonfiction books with a focus on sports, ghosts and haunted places, and graphic novels. Matt lives in New York.